Emmy
the Exaggerating Elephant

Fenton
the Fearful Frog

Gertie
the Grungy Goat

Herbie
the Happy Hamster

Ivy
the Impatient Iguana

D0576433

Ollie
the Obedient Ostrich

Perry
the Polite Porcupine

Queenie
the Quiet Quail

Rupert
the Resourceful Rhinoceros

Wendy
the Wise Woodchuck

Xavier
the X-ploring Xenops

Yori
the Yucky Yak

Ziggy
the Zippy Zebra

NOTE TO PARENTS

Herbie's Happy Day
A story about positive thinking

In this story, Herbie the Happy Hamster makes the best of a series of mishaps when his friends come to visit on a stormy day. Despite a leak in the roof and other accidents caused by the storm, Herbie maintains his sunny disposition and shows his AlphaPet friends how to keep their spirits up.

In addition to enjoying this delightful story with your child, you can use it to teach a gentle lesson about the important value of positive thinking—making the best of things and thinking of ways to cope with challenges.

You can also use this story to introduce the letter **H**. As you read about Herbie the Happy Hamster, ask your child to listen for all the **H** words and point to the objects that begin with **H**. When you've finished reading the story, your child will enjoy doing the activity at the end of the book.

The AlphaPets™ characters were conceived and created by Ruth Lerner Perle.
Characters interpreted and designed by Deborah Colvin Borgo.
Cover/book design and production by Norton & Company.
Logo design by Deborah Colvin Borgo and Nancy S. Norton.
Grolier Books is a Division of Grolier Enterprises, Inc.   Printed and Manufactured in the United States of America

Herbie's
Happy Day

RUTH LERNER PERLE

Illustrated by Judy Blankenship

GROLIER
B O O K S

One stormy spring morning, Herbie the Happy
Hamster was preparing a delicious lunch for some of
his AlphaPet friends. He made big juicy hamburgers
with pickles and onions. And he spread honey on slices
of homemade bread. Then he put all the food neatly
on the table.

"Mmm," said Herbie. "My friends will enjoy nice hot
hamburgers on this rainy, windy day."

Soon the doorbell rang, and Herbie ran to let his friends in.

"What a horrible, horrible day," complained Una the Unhappy Unicorn. "Rainy days are so sad and gloomy."

"Be happy that you have that big umbrella and those warm rubber boots. They kept you dry!" said Herbie.

"Oh dear, just look at my hat!" cried Perry the Polite Porcupine. "I'm afraid it got all wet!"

"Be happy that your hat didn't fall off your head!" said Herbie. "The wind might have blown it away!"

"Listen to the wind howl. I wish it would stop!" declared Delilah the Demanding Duck.

"Cheer up, everyone! Be happy!" said Herbie. "Think of the good side—rain makes flowers grow!"

As they hung up their coats, Una noticed drops of rain trickling from the ceiling.

Plink, plink, plink.

"Oh dear, oh dear," cried Una. "There's a hole in your roof!"

"So there is!" said Herbie. "I'll have to fix it, but don't worry. I'll collect the rainwater in this bucket. It's the best kind of water for shampooing, you know! And the raindrops make such a pretty sound. Just like the music my harp makes."

"Music, shmusic! I'm hungry! Let's eat!" said Delilah.

The AlphaPets went into the kitchen and sat down at the table.

"Everything looks and smells so delicious," said Perry, as he placed a napkin in his lap. "Please pass the hamburgers and that nice bread."

Herbie was just about to serve the hamburgers when—

Crack! A huge branch came crashing through the glass door and fell against the table! The rain came pouring in and leaves and sand were scattered everywhere.

"The house is falling in! The house is falling in!" shouted Delilah.

"Oh dear, oh dear!" cried Una.

"This *is* most upsetting," added Perry, folding his napkin neatly.

"Phew!" sighed Herbie. "Let's be happy that no one is hurt."

"Look at all this water!" shouted Delilah. "Your house will be flooded if the door stays open!"

"We'd better pull this branch out of the way," agreed Herbie. "Then we can close the door."

"Let's all grab hold of the branch and pull together!" Herbie said.

"The branch is too heavy," said Delilah. "It's too much work."

"But it's good exercise!" Herbie answered. "It will make your muscles big and strong. Come on, everybody, pull! Heave ho!"

So the AlphaPets pulled and pulled until the branch was out of the way and they could close the door.

"Hurray!" shouted Herbie. "Be happy! We did it! And this branch will make good firewood for my fireplace."

"How can we be happy? Look at our lunch! It's ruined," Una sighed.

"Do you have anything else to eat?" asked Delilah.

Herbie opened the refrigerator.

"There's nothing in there!" cried Delilah. "Just a half-empty jar of honey and some lemons."

"Nothing there! How can you say that?" cried Herbie. "We have a jar half-*full* of delicious honey and the freshest, ripest, juiciest lemons. "We can make a pitcher of lemonade. So, be happy."

Herbie hummed a happy tune as he squeezed the lemons, and mixed the juice with honey and water.

He poured glasses of lemonade for everyone. Then he smiled and said, "Let's all sit around the fire to keep warm and dry. When the rain stops, I'll treat you all to hamburgers at Harriet's Heavenly Hamburger Hut."

Herbie played his harmonica while the AlphaPets sat around the fire drinking their lemonade.

Before long, the wind died down. Herbie looked out the window.

"Hey! Hey! Hey!" said Herbie. "It stopped raining! Hooray! Now, just as soon as I patch the hole in the roof, we can head for the Hamburger Hut."

Herbie ran to get his ladder and his tool chest. When he returned, his AlphaPet friends were all ready, waiting to help him.

Everyone held the ladder as Herbie climbed up and hammered a wooden shingle neatly in place. But when he started to nail the second shingle, Herbie's hammer slipped and he hit his finger.

"Ouch!" cried Herbie.

"Oh, Herbie!" said Perry. "Are you bleeding?"

"No, I just bruised my finger." Herbie answered. "I'm happy that I didn't hurt my whole hand."

"All I have to do now," said Herbie, "is paint the patch, and the roof will be as good as new."

The AlphaPets watched as Herbie opened a can of paint, dipped his brush in, and painted the new shingles on the roof.

But when Herbie leaned back to admire his work, his foot slipped and the paint tipped over.

Splash! Green paint splattered and dripped all over the side of the house.

"Oh, how horrible!" said Una. "Look at the mess!"

"I'm afraid you'll have to repaint the whole house now," Perry suggested.

Herbie climbed down the ladder and looked at the spattered wall.

"Hmm, I don't have enough paint for the whole house, but I do have a little," Herbie said. "And I have a good idea. Just watch! I'll have the happiest house in AlphaPet Corners."

Everyone watched as Herbie dipped his brush into his paints. First the red, then the purple, then the orange and the pink.

The AlphaPets could hardly believe their eyes.

Herbie had turned the green paint drips into a beautiful flower garden!

"You see," Herbie said with a great, sunny smile, "the wind and showers really did bring us flowers."

The AlphaPets laughed and cheered as the sun came out.

Then Herbie jingled the coins in his purse and said, "Now we can all go down to the Hamburger Hut and have one of Harriet's heavenly hamburgers. Follow me!"

"Hey, hey, hey! Don't worry, be happy!" whooped the AlphaPets as they hopped down the hill and into town.

"Things always turn out for the best. Especially when you work to make them better," said Herbie. "This has been a hectic, happy day."

Everyone, even Una, agreed. They each gave Herbie a big hug and said, "You're our happy hero, Herbie."

I hope you'll enjoy these happy words with me.

hammer

heart

harmonica

hook

hat

hammock

harp

hanger

hamburger

horn

Look back at the pictures in this book and try to find these and other things that begin with the letter H.

Know Your
Alphabet

Aa Bb

Gg Hh

Mm Nn Oo Pp

Uu Vv Ww